The Mountain Challenge

The Mountain Challenge

Bear Grylls
Illustrated by Emma McCann

Bear Grylls

To the young survivor
reading this book for the first time.
May your eyes always be wide open
to adventure, and your heart full
of courage and determination to
see your dreams through.

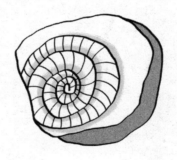

1

BUBBLE RUN

Lily held her breath and watched Mia send the shuttlecock soaring through the air. Down, down, down it went, towards a part of the court that nobody was standing in.

Just as Lily was about to shout "Yes!" in triumph, Callum came charging out of nowhere and swiped furiously with his racket. The shuttlecock flew low over the net back to Lily's side, and hit the ground before anyone could get it.

"Point!" Callum shouted. "He shoots, he scores!"

He led his team in an annoying victory dance, while Lily stared.

"It touched the ground on your side!" Mia protested. "It's not your point!"

"Did not!" Callum shouted. "I got it just before!"

Mia waved her racket at Lily.

"Lily! You were closest! Go on, tell him!"

"I, um ..." Lily began. She was ninety-nine percent sure Mia was right. The shuttlecock had touched the ground and Callum had scooped it up. All eyes swung towards her. She flushed.

"I, uh, I think ..." she stammered.

"See? Lily says it didn't land!" Callum called.

"That isn't what she said!" Mia snorted. "Did you, Lily? You saw it touch, right?"

"Um …"

Lily knew whatever she said was going to upset someone. Callum and Mia both looked mad. And now she was upsetting herself. She hated not being able to stand up to people. She hated letting them down even more.

"I've got to go!" she said as she ran from the court. "I don't want to be late!"

*

The moment Lily saw it, she thought the Bubble Run looked like serious fun. Everyone was paired up and strapped inside giant transparent inflatable bubbles, which raced along a sandy track that ran around the edge of a clearing at the top of the woods. They had to roll themselves along, trying not to hit other teams or anything else. Lily had been looking forward to it all week and now it was her turn.

There was a crowd of people waiting in front of Lily, including Mia. Lily hoped she wasn't upset with her, but hung back just in case. She pushed her hands into her pockets, slouching at the back of the group.

What was that in her pocket? Oh yes, a compass. She'd gotten it the day before, from Harry after they'd played Frisbee.

Harry had been playing to win, but he'd scared her by playing so hard, so he'd given her the compass as a gift to say sorry. At the time Lily had wondered why he thought she might want a compass, but she was too scared to say anything.

Just then the bubbles bounced into view through the trees, with a leader firmly strapped inside each one. Lily forgot about the compass and listened carefully as the leaders clambered out and explained how the activity worked.

"Each bubble takes two of you. Strap into this harness – it's very important that you *double* strap for safety. If you come loose inside the bubble you could get hurt. To move the bubble you both have to lean yourselves in the direction you want it to move – and it goes!

So, choose a partner, and we'll send you around the course in pairs."

"Come with me, Lily?" Mia said to Lily, with a friendly smile. Lily beamed back. It was good to know Mia wasn't upset with her after all.

"Sure!"

Lily and Mia watched the first two pairs go around the track. Everyone cheered and laughed as the bubbles spun and wobbled and bounced. Eventually they rolled back to the start and the giddy kids were let out, laughing and dizzy.

Next up were Lily and Mia, and Joe and Omar. They got inside the bubbles and the leaders fitted the inflatable hatch to seal them in. The sides were a bit cloudy, but Lily could make out everything outside. Mia was fiddling with her straps and then stopped. She hadn't done up the second set.

"It's too uncomfortable to do both. I've done this before, it's fine with just one anyway … we're ready!" she called out loudly to the leader waiting for their signal.

But we were told it was important! Lily wanted to say. But Mia seemed so confident.

Just then the leaders gave their bubble a push, and they were off.

The whole world spun around them. Lily felt her head and her stomach whirling and swirling. She suddenly understood why they had been told not to have a big breakfast.

The girls soon got the hang of it. You just had to lean a little, and you could make the bubble go forward, or tilt it to the left or the right.

"Here come the boys," Mia called.

Joe and Omar's bubble was bouncing towards them.

"Are they trying to ram us?" Lily could hear the tremble in her voice.

It was against the rules for bubbles to ram each other deliberately, but it looked like that was what Joe and Omar were about to do. Lily hadn't thought either of the boys was the kind who would break the rules but …

Bump.

The bubbles collided.

The inflatable hulls took the impact, but both bubbles got knocked off course.

Lily saw the gap in the trees spinning around ahead of them. They were heading for a slope.

"Mia, we need to go right!"

"Got it!"

Mia and Lily leaned their bodies over to the right to get their bubble back on course.

Bump.

The boys hit them again.

The girls' bubble spun around so that Mia was hanging down from the top.

And then, with the sound of ripping Velcro, Mia's single strap came loose.

"Aargh!"

Mia couldn't fight gravity. She tumbled down and landed on Lily.

"Ow!" Lily shouted.

Lily was double-strapped in place, but the girls were tangled up together and the bubble was seriously unbalanced. Lily felt it teeter over towards the edge of the hill.

"Mia, get up! You've got to –"

It was too late. The bubble tipped over the edge ...

Instantly the world started spinning. Lily's head was shaken this way and that as the bubble tumbled its way down the slope. Picking up speed with every second, bouncing higher and higher. It was totally out of control.

2

HIGH AND MIGHTY

Mia screamed as she tumbled around inside the bubble. Lily's stomach went into free fall.

"Oof!"

"Ow!"

Mia and Lily crunched in a massive crash as the bubble hit the ground one last time before coming to a stop. In the crush, the compass that was still in Lily's pocket jabbed painfully into her.

Lily pulled it out as Mia climbed off her.

"Oops!" Mia looked like she didn't know whether to giggle or cry.

Lily wasn't laughing and she definitely wanted to cry. It had really *hurt* to have Mia land on her so many times. But instead of checking herself for injuries, Lily couldn't stop staring at the compass in her hand. Its needle was spinning around and around, and she could swear there were five directions on it. It was obviously broken. Was Harry going to be annoyed with her for breaking it?

The whole going-out-of-control thing wouldn't have happened if Mia had just followed instructions and done up the double strap in the first place. And now she'd broken Harry's compass.

But Lily still didn't say anything. She wanted to stay friends, not cause any more trouble.

"Come on," Mia said. "Let's get out of here, Lily."

Lily was nearest to the hatch. She just had to twist a couple of toggles, and give it a push. She started to crawl out.

"Aargh!"

Suddenly Lily was tumbling down a rocky slope. Small stones and pebbles rained down next to her.

At last Lily bumped into something that stopped her. But whatever it was made of was so hard that it knocked the breath out of her. She lay absolutely still, eyes shut, until she was positive she had stopped moving. The bubble must have come to a halt at the top of a ditch. When she'd opened the hatch, she hadn't checked to see if there was actually any ground outside.

Lily climbed to her feet and dusted herself off.

"Well, that was really smart, wasn't it?" she started to mutter.

But the words dried in her mouth as

she saw where she was.

Lily slowly turned on the spot.

There was no ditch.

There was no sign of the bubble.

There was no sign of Mia.

In fact, there was no sign of camp.

The slope she had fallen down was as long as a soccer field, and as steep as the roof of a house. It was covered in rocks and boulders. Lily had bumped into one of them. A few feet farther on, the slope plunged over a sheer drop.

But that was only the start of the weirdness.

Lily looked out over a sea of mountains and deep valleys. Some of the lower slopes seemed to be covered in forest. The tops were all bare, jagged rock. It stretched out away from her like an ocean.

A cold wind was blowing, and it cut right through Lily's thin T-shirt. She shivered, and wrapped her arms around herself and rubbed them to try to keep warm. Then she lifted her eyes.

However she had gotten here, Lily could see that she needed to get off this high ground and out of this wind. She ran her eyes along the tops of the mountains.

Over to the side, the slope turned into a flat ridge that she could walk along. In fact, she thought she could see a route from the ridge, down a spur of high ground and into the valley below. Okay, she decided. That was where she should go.

But it was easier said than done. The first thing she had to do was step away from her safe little rock. The slope was steep and dangerous. She'd have to be careful with every step.

Lily decided the best way would be to crawl across the slope, sideways, on all fours.

She cautiously put one foot out, then a hand, then the other hand, and then the other foot. Crawling slowly towards the ridge, she didn't look down.

The thought of the drop behind her was just too scary.

Suddenly a stone gave way beneath her. Lily's foot shot away and she dropped down onto one knee, banging it against the hard ground. She heard the loose stone tumble away, until suddenly there was silence as it went over the edge.

Lily's heart was beating faster than ever and she wanted to cry. But she knew she had to go on. Slowly, she straightened her leg and started to crawl again.

She moved carefully for a while, but as the ridge came closer, she decided to risk it and move a little faster.

Bad move. Her foot slipped away again and this time she fell flat on her

face. Worse, Lily could feel herself start to slide down the slope. She tried to dig her fingers and feet into the rocky earth, but it was no good. Soon she started to roll. She was out of control.

Lily was spinning and bumping towards the sheer drop.

3

ROCKY RENDEZVOUS

"Put your arms and legs out!"

A man was shouting. Lily could hear him over the rattle of falling stones and her own panic.

"Put your arms and legs out! *Quickly!*"

Lily flung her arms and legs into a starfish position.

She kept skidding down, but at least she'd stopped rolling. Soon she could feel herself slowing. At last, once she had stopped moving, Lily lay flat on her back and breathed. She didn't dare to move.

"Are you okay?" the man called.

Lily just couldn't find her voice. She knew she needed to speak, but she couldn't.

"Are you okay? Can you come back towards me?" the man called again.

Lily looked. She had stopped just before a sheer drop. She panicked again, feeling the drop pull at her like a magnet. If she moved, she would go over it.

"I … I don't think I can," she called back eventually, fighting to keep her voice steady. "Okay. Hold on."

Boots scuffed on rock. She watched the man come into view, backward, holding on to a rope. He was dressed for the mountains, in tough pants, a protective helmet and a colorful anorak.

He stopped a short distance away from her.

"Okay, this is as far as the rope goes. So I'm going to have to ask you to be brave and do this yourself. I'll tell you what to do."

Lily nodded. She didn't feel brave, though.

"Great stuff. Okay, first, you need to roll over onto your front." Lily didn't need to be told twice. She knew that she was in trouble and she trusted the man, whoever he was. "That's it," he said as she twisted herself slowly over. "Well done. You're doing great."

Lily carried on doing exactly what he told her, turning around until she was pointing up the slope, then carefully edging herself along towards him, only moving one hand or foot at a time.

It took all her courage, but Lily managed to follow his directions. She took it slowly and surely. Eventually she was close enough for him to pull her to her feet.

"Excellent! Now, go in front of me and hold on to the rope while we work our way back up …"

A few minutes later, they were both

on flat ground. The man started to coil his rope up and put it in his backpack.

"So, how did you get there?" he asked with a friendly smile.

Lily wasn't quite sure how to answer. She stayed quiet.

The man looked at her kindly.

"Pretty scary, huh? Don't worry, I know how it feels. Listen, my name's Bear, and I'm exploring a new path over the mountains … and now it looks like you're joining me. Are you ready for some adventure?"

Lily looked out over the endless mountaintops. She wasn't so sure that she wanted an adventure. Mostly, she wanted it all to be over and to be back at camp.

But she could see there wasn't any other way off this mountain.

"Thanks for helping me, Bear," she said at last. "I'm Lily."

"Pleased to meet you, Lily." Bear started to dig around inside his backpack. "You'll need some gear for the mountains. Those pants are fine – lightweight and rugged. But let's get you some more clothes to go on top of that T-shirt. We both need to be wearing lots of thin layers, so the air between them gets warmed up by body heat."

Bear produced a shirt from his

backpack. "This one's good …"

Lily was about to take it when he pulled out another.

"Or how about this?"

He laid the two shirts on a rock, and rummaged in his backpack again.

"And there's these …"

Eventually, Lily was looking at a pile of shirts, sweatshirts, anoraks and hats.

"Choose whatever you like," Bear told her cheerfully.

Lily stared at all the choices. She had to make a decision. She *hated* making decisions. She almost felt as nervous as she had when she was tumbling down the slope.

"I don't know," Lily stammered. "Um … which do you think, Bear?"

Bear's eyes were kind.

"You don't have to worry about getting it wrong, Lily," he said gently. "All that matters is that you feel comfortable wearing them. They have to be right for *you*."

Lily felt a bit bolder. She chose a couple of shirts, a sweatshirt, jacket and hat.

"Great choices," Bear approved. "You'll need a helmet and these boots, too, instead of sneakers."

He put down a helmet and a pair of scuffed, leather mountain boots. Lily put the helmet and boots on, and bounced on her toes a couple of times. They seemed to grip her feet and her ankles. She felt herself planted firmly on the rocky ground.

"Thanks, they feel good," she said.

Bear was looking out over the mountains.

"Great. So now that you're set, we need to head out. You should always try to take the easiest route off a mountain, which is back the way I came." He pointed. "We need to get down to the valley, where it's warmer, and we've got more chance of finding shelter and food. It's always best to come down a mountain spur, if you can, because you get a view down in all directions, and you can get a good idea of where you're going. So, if we follow this flat ground, then we come to that ridge, then follow that spur, which leads down ..."

In fact, Bear was describing exactly the route that Lily had worked out for herself. She wanted to tell him so, but she felt worried about speaking up. So Lily just kept quiet. Still, she was pleased to know she had gotten it right. And it felt good to know where they were going. Hopefully she would be back at camp before too long.

They both took a drink of water from Bear's water bottle, and ate half an energy bar each.

"Just enough to give us energy for now," Bear said. "We'll take a break every hour – five minutes, to stop us stiffening up – and then we'll have a real meal break in a few hours. Does that sound okay, Lily?"

Lily was looking at the ground, but she nodded.

"Then let's go!"

They set off together towards the ridge. Soon they reached a point where their path ahead was a ledge that was only ten or twelve feet wide. On one side was a massive cliff face that towered above them. On the other was another sheer drop.

"That's where I came across," Bear said. "How are you with heights, Lily?"

The ledge was wide enough to walk along without going near the edge.

"I guess I'm okay, as long as I don't think I'm going to fall down one!" Lily said truthfully, looking at it.

"Good girl! Let's go then."

Lily followed behind Bear, feeling confident for the first time since this whole strange adventure began.

But then a colossal creaking, groaning sound filled the air. Lily could feel the noise vibrating in the ground and in her stomach.

"It's going!" Bear shouted. "Get back, quick!"

They dashed back the way they had come. The groaning grew louder. Thirty feet ahead of them, a whole chunk of mountain, the size of a house, fell away.

4

HIGH SEAS

A cloud of dust and stone rose up as the rock face hit the floor of the valley with a mighty crash. Lily dared to peek over the edge.

"Was that our fault?" Lily gasped. She was always prepared to own up to anything she had done wrong, but she didn't want to think she had been responsible for destroying a whole mountain.

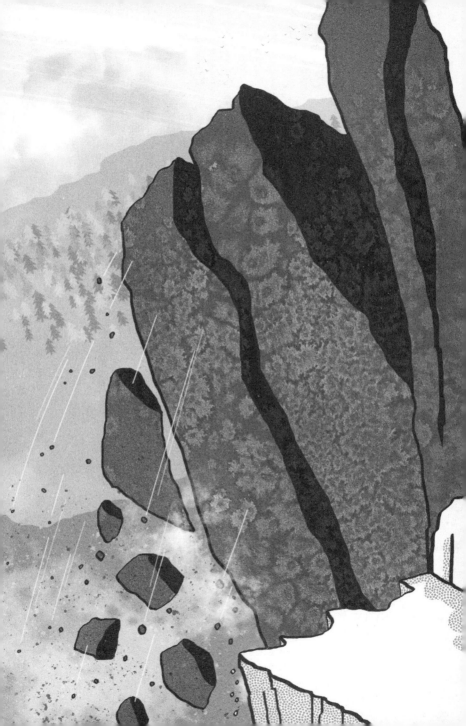

Bear shook his head with a smile.

"These mountains are millions of years old. It would have been some little crack that's just gotten bigger and bigger over the centuries – until, today, it suddenly decided it couldn't hold the weight anymore."

"Phew!"

That was a relief, but it was the only good news.

Lily and Bear couldn't go any farther along the ledge. The chunk had taken a massive bite out of it.

"So – um, Bear – are we stranded up here?"

"There will be other ways down," Bear promised. "I said that was the easiest way, not the *only* way. Now we just have to find the second easiest.

But hey – look at this."

Several large rocks had dropped down at the same time as the chunk of mountain. Bear passed Lily a stone the size of her fist. There was a spiral pattern embedded in it, like a coiled-up shellfish.

"Wow, a fossil!" Lily exclaimed.

"This guy was once swimming around in a prehistoric ocean," Bear agreed. "Then he died and sank to the bottom. He got up here because the seabed has raised itself about a millimeter per year, for millions of years. *That's* how old the mountains are."

"Cool." Lily looked at it with wonder.

"Keep it as a souvenir," Bear suggested.

"There'll be plenty more."

"Thanks." Lily slipped it into her pocket. "So, what's the second-easiest way down?"

"This way," Bear smiled, and they set off.

Lily knew Bear had already explored the area, but she still felt nervous. The only way out was to go back to the slope where he had rescued her. What if she fell again?

Lily tried to get the words out several times to ask Bear. Each time they just dried up in her mouth. She didn't want Bear to think she was making a fuss.

Lily was very relieved when they walked past the spot where she had met Bear, and kept going. She kept a careful side-eye on the steep, rocky slope, until it was out of sight.

But they soon came to another slope. This one ran from the base of a tall cliff, down to an area of flatter ground below. In between, the surface was covered with thousands of small, fist-sized rocks.

"All those rocks came off the cliff, I guess?" Lily asked.

Bear nodded.

"It's called scree and it's something else that happens over millions of years. It's very loose and unstable – and unfortunately we have to get down it. The best way is to take it fast."

Lily thought again of the slippery slope where she'd first met Bear. Lily didn't like the idea of going down anywhere fast. She took a deep breath and plucked up the courage to speak.

"Um, Bear … wouldn't it be safer to take it nice and slow?"

Bear stopped and smiled. "It seems like that would be a good idea, doesn't it?" Bear agreed. "But if we went slow, all those loose stones and rocks would come down beside us and we might get swept away with them. So we take big, confident steps and keep the weight on our heels we so that we don't overbalance forward." He grinned at Lily, who carried on staring at the slope. "If you do begin to slip, try to turn sideways. That will help you balance, and not fall onto your back. But just keep going, Lily, and you'll be fine!"

Bear set off, taking long strides and holding his arms out for balance. The slope was so steep that he kicked his legs out into thin air with every step. Lily waited until she was sure she had the hang of it, and set off after him.

It was tough going. Lily did her best to copy Bear, but all the loose rocks made it impossible to get a firm footing. Every step set off smaller slides of rocks. The slope was steep, but Lily didn't stumble.

She put her weight on her heels and planted every step firmly before she took the next one. It felt like no time at all before they both were down at the bottom. A few loose pebbles trickled down after them, but that was it.

Lily smiled triumphantly at Bear, who smiled back.

"Fantastic, Lily! You looked really confident as you came down. And we cut a hundred feet off our descent," said Bear. "Now, let's see how to get down from here. I haven't been here before so we'll be exploring together."

Bear and Lily soon worked out the ways to get down. But it wasn't great news. They had three options.

Go back up the scree slope.

Climb up a nearly vertical cliff, as high

as several houses stacked on top of each other.

Or get down the cliff on the other side.

Bear and Lily stood side by side on the edge of the cliff, looking down.

"See?" Bear said. "We can go down in a couple of stages. There's a ridge down there, and another below that one. Then we can rejoin that spur we were heading for. This is definitely the way to go."

Lily peered down the drop. Was it *really* the easiest way?

Lily knew she needed to speak up.

If she didn't say anything then Bear might think she was good at climbing.

If she did say something then he might think she was being awkward.

Help!

5

DOUBLE UP

Bear had put his backpack down on the ground, and was pulling out his rope. He noticed that Lily had gone very quiet.

"What are you thinking about, Lily?" he asked.

Lily's mind whirled. It would be so easy to tell Bear she wasn't worrying about anything, but she didn't want to lie. So she did what she usually did and said nothing at all.

Bear smiled gently.

"You know, Lily, when you're working together, everyone on a team needs to know exactly what everyone else can do. It can be a matter of survival for both of us. So, if you feel you can't do something, don't feel bad about telling me."

"Well…" she said, her voice shaky. "I haven't really done this kind of climbing before." Lily thought of the climbing wall at camp. "Well, maybe just a little bit."

Bear nodded and pulled out something that looked like a lot of canvas loops all sewn together. Lily recognized it. It was good to see something familiar.

"That's a climbing harness, yeah?"

"Got it in one. Can you put it on?" Bear asked.

"Sure," she said. Lily remembered enough from camp to do that. She could feel her confidence growing a little.

The big loop went around her waist, and her legs went through a couple of smaller loops that were tied to it. Meanwhile, Bear did his own harness up, and tightened his helmet. "Got to protect your head," he said. "It's the only one you've got." Lily made sure her helmet was fastened properly too.

Next, Bear pulled out a steel metal loop. One side was hinged, so that it could snap open and shut. Lily recognized that too.

"And that's a… carabiner?"

"Bingo!" said Bear. "You've got a really good memory, Lily."

Bear fixed the carabiner onto a buckle on the front of Lily's harness. Then he took out a gadget that looked like a metal *8*, with different sized loops. He snapped one of the loops onto the carabiner.

"And do you know what this is?" he said. Lily half nodded, though she couldn't quite remember the actual word. "It's a descender – it's what you use to control yourself as you go down. I'll put an autoblock on the rope below it, and that'll slow you down even more if you go too fast. All you need to remember is that your right hand is your guide hand and your left is the brake hand. Hold the rope above the descender with your guide hand, and you keep your brake hand on the autoblock. If you let go, the autoblock digs into the rope and stops you."

Lily nodded. It was a lot to take in, but she thought she could do it.

"Right hand to guide, left hand to slow me down," she said.

"You've got it!" Bear smiled, and peered over the edge. "Now then, this is a fifty-meter rope, so it should be long enough if we do this in stages."

Bear whacked some metal pegs into the rock with a hammer, and attached a carabiner to each one. Then he ran the rope through both of the carabiners. He pulled on the ends of the rope until it was exactly halfway through the two. Last of all, he ran the two halves of the rope together through Lily's descender.

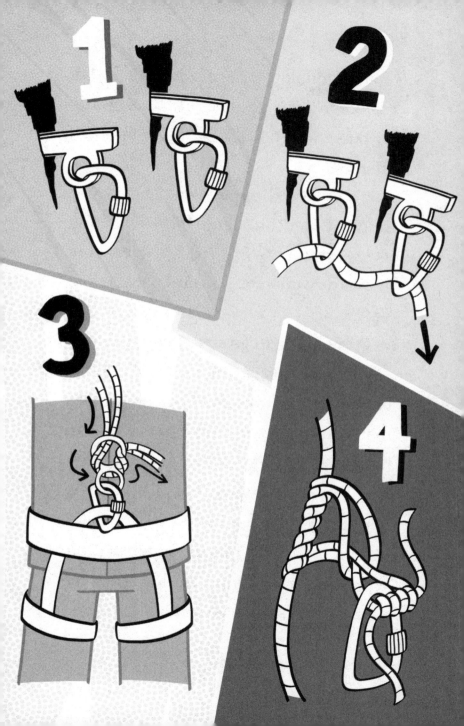

"We double it up," he said. "So, once I'm down after you, I'll just have to tug on one end, and it will all come down after us."

Lily's jaw dropped and her heart thudded. Her confidence had been doing okay – until now. She tried to speak, but no words came. But she knew she had to say it…

"Am I going to go first?" she asked.

"Yes," Bear said quietly. "Only one of us can go at a time, and I can only check that you're fastened on right if I'm up here with you before you go. But you're a lot braver than you think, Lily. I know you can do this."

Bear started to put the autoblock on, wrapping a red nylon cord around the rope. Lily was so nervous that she wanted to do something to take her mind off it.

"I think I can remember how to do that," Lily told Bear.

And she could. She coiled the red cord around the rope four or five times, and remembered to make sure that none of the loops crossed over another.

Bear smiled.

"Absolutely perfect! You're a natural, Lily!"

Then it was time to go. Lily's heart still pounded as she turned her back on the drop. She leaned herself back, and started to walk down the cliff.

The rope ran easily through the descender. There was no knot to stop her falling. It was just friction that stopped her sliding straight down and hitting the ground at the speed of gravity.

But it all went well. Lily just kept walking backward down the cliff, and before long she was standing on the ledge below.

A couple of minutes later, Bear was standing next to her.

"You're great at this!" he said cheerfully. He tugged on one end of the rope. The other end shot up back the way they had come and through the two carabiners in the rock above them. A moment later, the whole rope dropped down at their feet. Bear hammered some more pegs into the rock and fastened the rope to them again.

The ledge sloped down before the next drop. Bear held on to the rope as he peered over the edge.

"Hmm."

"Is there a problem?" Lily asked nervously.

"Well, this is an overhang. The ledge sticks out from the mountain. You won't be able to walk down the cliff, like you just did. You'll be hanging in mid-air. But everything else works the same."

"That's fine," Lily said, suddenly feeling a lot more confident. The first time hadn't been a problem, so she could do this too.

Once again Lily found herself back out over a drop. Once she was past the overhang, the cliff face was a few feet in front of her. Lily hung vertically on the rope.

But just like before, the rope glided smoothly through her descender. Soon she was standing on a new ledge. She felt great. She was getting the hang of this.

Bear joined her again and looked down. Lily saw his face suddenly go thoughtful.

"Okay," he said. "This might not be so good."

Lily couldn't see what the problem was. This ledge looked just the same as the last one. Flat bit of rock, cliff face, drop …

Then she stood next to Bear and looked over the edge.

"That's a long way down," Lily said. "It looks … um, I mean … is it more than fifty meters?"

Bear nodded.

"I'd say a hundred. I miscalculated. It's too long for our fifty-meter rope, even if we don't double it up."

"So …" Lily didn't like what she was thinking. She looked up at the sixty foot drop they had just come down. And the overhang at the top.

Even if they could climb back up the cliff, they would have to hang upside down as they got over the overhang.

"Are we going back up?" she whispered.

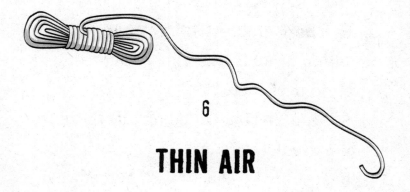

6

THIN AIR

"No," Bear replied, to Lily's relief. "We're done climbing up and down, for the moment."

He pointed along the ridge. "Now, we're going to climb along. That way."

The ridge got narrower at the end, like the cliff face was sucking it back in. Eventually there wasn't any more ridge at all, just cliff. It curved out of sight, so Lily couldn't see the end of it, but she could see flat ground beyond the cliff.

"So," Lily said nervously, just to be sure she'd understood. "We're going to climb around this cliff to get to that ground over there?"

She couldn't help noticing that the cliff was extremely vertical.

Bear smiled. "That's exactly what we'll be doing."

Lily opened her mouth to say that she really wasn't very comfortable with that idea.

Then she closed it again because it would just be easier to go along with what Bear said.

But then she remembered what Bear had said about everyone on the team needing to know exactly what everyone else could do. Bear needed to know this.

Telling the truth wasn't making a fuss. In fact, *not* making a fuss would be like lying.

"Um. I haven't done any climbing like this before, Bear," Lily said. "All my climbing on the wall was up and down."

"Well, that's worth knowing, thank you," Bear said seriously. "Fortunately we have two things that are really going to help us. First, the right equipment. We'll still be attached to the rope, and the rope will be attached to the rock. Have a look at this."

Bear pulled a bundle of gadgets out of his backpack. They looked like some strange martial arts toys. Each one had three or four jagged, curved bits of metal on the end of a metal rod.

He pushed one into a crack in the cliff, and released a switch. Inside the crack, the blades all sprang apart with a *snick*.

"This is a cam," said Bear. "Try to pull it out."

Lily took it with both hands and pulled with all her strength. The cam stayed exactly where it was. Bear pressed the switch again and the blades retracted, and then Lily could pull it out easily.

"Like you just saw, when it's in a crack, the blades make sure it stays there," Bear said. "And that's what the rope will be attached to."

"That's neat." Lily handed the cam back. "What's the other thing that will help us?"

Bear smiled.

"The right people. People with the ability to keep their heads and do what's needed. And I believe that's you. You're great at keeping calm under pressure, Lily."

Lily felt herself blush a little. Could it be true? She kind of liked the idea of being seen that way.

Bear carried on. "Here's the plan. I'll climb along the cliff to the level ground first. I'll take one end of the rope with me and leave a row of these cams along the way, with the rope going through them. You'll be fastened to the other end of the rope. When I'm across, you follow. If you slip then the rope will hold you. Every time you come to a cam, just release it and hang it on your harness. You'll still be held by the rope and cams in front of you. And you keep going."

"Okay." Lily was reassured by how the cam had just stayed stuck in the crack, even when she yanked on it really hard. And Bear's confidence in her abilities gave her confidence in herself. "Let's do this," she said, smiling.

Bear fastened one end of the rope to a carabiner on his harness, and the other end to a carabiner on hers. In between, the rope lay coiled on the ground. Then Bear jammed the first cam into the cliff, right at the edge, and clipped a carabiner hanging on the end of its handle onto his rope. He started to climb out. The rope uncoiled slowly from where it was lying on the rock. Lily kept a close eye on where Bear was going as he picked out the footholds in the cliff. She was going to have to take the same route. She noticed Bear was following the same rule as when he guided her off that rocky slope, only moving one hand or foot at a time. She told herself that was what she would do.

Every few feet, Bear put a new cam into the rock and clipped it onto the rope. Soon he was around the curve of the cliff and out of sight. But the rope kept paying out, and Lily heard the clicking of the cams.

"Okay, I'm here!" Bear called eventually. "I'm going to take up the slack."

The coiled rope suddenly paid out a lot more quickly, as Bear pulled it in from his side. Then there was a gentle tug on Lily's harness. The rope now went straight from her, through the row of cams, and around the cliff to Bear.

"Okay," Bear called again. "It's ready for you!"

Lily's heart was pounding again, but she was ready for the challenge.

"Coming!" she called back. She stepped off the safety of the ridge.

She was glad she had told Bear she hadn't done this before. It meant that Bear had set this up so that she could climb across without any experience.

If she hadn't said anything, perhaps he might have picked a harder way of doing it. She could have ended up putting them both in danger. Speaking up had been the best thing to do.

Lily could feel all the empty air behind her. It would provide exactly zero support if she fell. They called it "thin air" for a reason. Every time she reached out with a foot or a hand for a new hold, she tested it carefully before putting her weight on it.

Soon, Lily had climbed around the curve in the cliff. She couldn't see the ridge she had come from. But she could see Bear, only a few feet away, smiling encouragingly at her. He was sitting on the rock, rope wrapped around his body, legs braced to hold her weight if she fell.

"Just a few more steps …" Bear said. He reached out to help her onto level ground. "And you've done it!"

While Bear coiled the rope up, Lily looked around.

They were on a spur of the mountain. It was a wide, flat ridge that wiggled and wound its way downward. And there weren't any more drops to deal with.

"No more climbing!" Lily said happily.

"Well," Bear smiled as he put the coiled-up rope back in his backpack, "hopefully not."

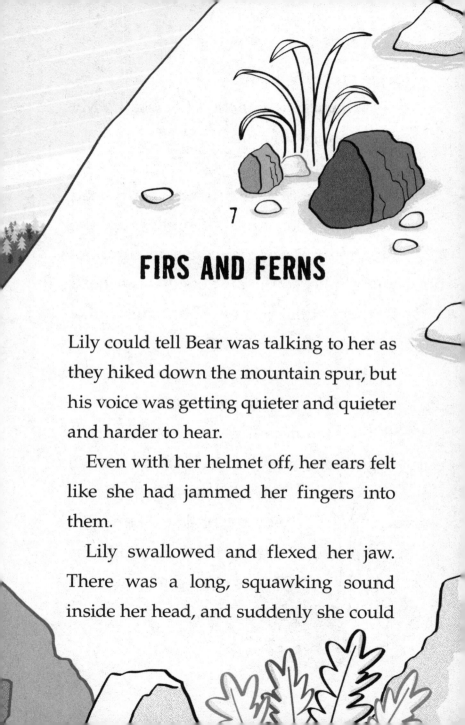

7

FIRS AND FERNS

Lily could tell Bear was talking to her as they hiked down the mountain spur, but his voice was getting quieter and quieter and harder to hear.

Even with her helmet off, her ears felt like she had jammed her fingers into them.

Lily swallowed and flexed her jaw. There was a long, squawking sound inside her head, and suddenly she could hear properly again.

"Whoa!" She clutched her head. "My ears popped, big time!"

Bear smiled.

"The air pressure inside your head was still the same as higher up the mountain. But we've come down about half a mile, so the air outside your head is much thicker now. That can make your ears feel blocked."

"It's warmer, too," Lily noticed. She unzipped the front of her anorak.

"The temperature goes up about four degrees for every thousand feet we come down," Bear said, "which is why the basic rule if you're stuck in the mountains is – get out of them as soon as you can."

They had been descending the spur for a couple of hours now. The ground was still steep, but not nearly as steep as it had been. They took a five-minute break every hour, as Bear had promised. Each time they ate a bit of one of the energy bars, and washed it down with water from the bottle.

Lily remembered that Bear had said it was best to come down a spur so you could see what was coming. Being on the high ground made her feel in control, and she liked it. She could see more valleys and lakes and rivers below them. There wouldn't be any surprises thrown at her.

"Anyway, sorry, what were you saying?" Lily asked.

Bear smiled.

"Just that we'll find a change from the energy bars in that forest."

They were coming to a pine forest that covered the sides and bottom of a valley, so that it looked like they were approaching a bowl of trees.

"There'll be berries and ferns …"

"We're going to eat ferns?" Lily asked in surprise.

"They're generally safe to eat, if you boil them," Bear assured her. "We'll find a stream to top up with fresh water. And berries. Blue or black berries are usually edible, white and yellow not. You can usually eat the tips and seeds of grasses too…"

As Bear spoke, a fantastic rainbow caught Lily's attention. It wasn't all washed out, like the ones she was used

to back home in the city. The colors were glowing and she could see the different bands very clearly. But didn't rainbows usually come after rain?

She was going to point it out to Bear, but she didn't want to interrupt.

"… and the basic rule is, don't use more energy finding food than you'll get back from it."

They reached the forest. The air was still and warm and smelled of pine. The bark on the tree nearest Bear was damaged and scratched at the height of his face, as if someone had attacked it with an axe. Bear rested his fingers on it for a moment, his face thoughtful. Lily was about to ask him about it when

Bear plucked off a piece of bark and passed it to her. He took another for himself, and started to eat it.

"You can eat all the parts of a fir tree, and also most bits of a pine," he said.

Lily was surprised, but she nibbled her own bit of bark as they walked on. It tasted – well, woody. But it wasn't exactly bad.

Soon they came to a stream tumbling fast through the trees, fresh off the mountain.

"And now we know exactly which way to go," Bear said.

"Because the stream knows the way out of the valley," Lily realized.

Bear smiled.

"Exactly! Follow water downstream and you always get somewhere."

In fact, the stream seemed eager to get out of the valley. It started to flow steeper and faster. Soon it was filling a ravine as wide as a main street back home. There wasn't room on the narrow banks for any trees, which were just wide enough for Lily and Bear to walk along.

They stopped for another five-minute break beside the frothing water, and Lily noticed a clump of ferns and remembered what Bear had said about eating them.

They finished off the water in Bear's bottles, and Bear filled them up from the stream.

"We don't know if there's anything dead upstream, so we'll boil it at our next stop, just to make sure it's free of nasties," he said. "And we'll treat ourselves to a real meal then too."

"Maybe we could take those ferns with us?" Lily asked. She pointed. "Oh, they've gone."

She couldn't see the ferns anywhere, which was silly. They had been right there. Then she realized why she couldn't see them.

"Oh. They're underwater!"

The stream had swollen up behind them. It was spilling out onto the banks where they had just been walking.

"Uh-oh."

Bear was looking up.

Lily raised her eyes above the level of the trees behind them.

The enormous mountain, which they had spent so long getting off, had vanished. The sky was a gray blur.

"Wow, that's a lot of rain!" Lily said.

"Too much rain," Bear said quickly. "And it's all coming our way. We have to get out of this ravine. It's a flash flood. A few more minutes and this whole place will be underwater."

8

TOO MUCH INFORMATION

Lily guessed that the only way out was down the ravine. But Bear put his hand on her shoulder straightaway.

"We can't go that way," he said. "It's flooding down there too. See?"

In front of them, the stream was already spilling over its banks.

"But we can walk through that," she said. It only looked ankle deep.

"It's still rising," Bear pointed out.

"It only takes six inches of fast-flowing water to move a parked car – and if it can move a car then it can move us."

The bank behind them was now completely underwater. If they couldn't go forward or backward, Lily thought, then they were cut off. So the only way out was …

She sighed and started to put on her helmet. "I guess we're climbing again!"

Bear smiled as he did his own helmet up, then bent down with his hands clasped together.

"Put your foot in here, and I'll boost you up to that ridge."

Lily clambered up the rocky side of the ravine, remembering the move-one-bit-at-a-time rule. Soon she was sitting on a ridge ten feet up from where they

had been. Bear scrambled up beside her. Lily peered down.

"Wow!"

The ravine was now wall-to-wall running water. The banks had vanished. A loose branch came zipping down on the surface. Lily would have had to run to keep up, it was moving so fast.

"Strange," Bear said. "I didn't see any of the usual signs for a storm."

"What are they?"

"Well, nature knows when it's coming." Bear ticked points off on his fingers. "So, spiders make their webs shorter and tighter, so they won't get washed away. Midges start to swarm. Plant smells get stronger as they open up to receive the water. And you often see rainbows before the rain because the air is already saturated. Of course, you don't always get all the signs, and some are harder to spot than others, but you'd expect to see a couple … Is something wrong?"

Lily's mouth had dropped open.

"I, um … I did see a rainbow," she admitted. "Earlier. But … um … I didn't think it was worth mentioning."

Bear smiled.

"It's not your fault, Lily. I'm the one who's meant to be guiding you. Just remember that for a survivor, there's no such thing as too much information. If it's true, if it's useful, just say it. If you see something unusual, it's always worth pointing it out."

After about an hour, the water had gone down enough for Lily and Bear to climb back down to the river. Soon after that they were out of the ravine and back in the pine forest. Up above, the clouds were turning red.

"We've got about two hours of daylight left," Bear said, checking his watch. "Waiting the flood out meant we didn't get as far as I'd hoped. I'm afraid we'll be spending the night in the forest. How are you with that?"

Lily looked at the trees around them. How would she feel, she wondered, in the dark and away from home?

Then she remembered.

"I've just spent all week at camp, so I think I'll be fine!" Lily answered. "We pitched our own tents in the woods."

Bear smiled.

"Great. We'll press on and find a good camping spot."

At their next break, Bear and Lily picked more bark off a fir tree. Bear also gathered handfuls of the needles together.

"We'll boil some of this up into a tea," he said. "It's full of vitamin C and will give us energy. And ... hello."

The tree also had those strange marks on the bark that Lily had noticed earlier. Again, Lily saw Bear eyeing them.

There's no such thing as too much information.

"What did that?" she asked.

"Well, that's bear sign," Bear said seriously. He smiled. "The animal kind. It was probably looking for insects under the bark."

"Bears?"

Lily looked quickly around. How big were bears? How close could one get in these trees without them seeing it?

"They're unavoidable out here, but you can deal with them," Bear assured her. "The one thing you don't do is try to outrun a bear because you can't. They can climb trees faster than you, too. If it's a brown bear – a grizzly – it will probably just be angry because you're in its territory, or you've come between a mother and her cubs. So, play dead. Lie down, curl up, do this to protect your neck …" Bear clasped both hands behind his neck. "And don't move. Once the bear has worked out you're not a threat, it'll move on. But this is mostly black bear territory, and unlike a grizzly, a black bear will attack because it's hungry, so lying down is not a good option. You have to face them down. Stand tall, wave your arms, jump, shout …"

Bear suddenly leaped forward, almost into her face. "And roar!"

Lily jumped.

Bear went back to his normal voice as Lily recovered from her surprise. "Like that. You really need to shout loudly."

"I'm not sure I could roar at a bear," Lily admitted. "I might just be too scared."

"Oh, it's terrifying," Bear agreed. "So you have to ask yourself some simple questions. Do I want to be a bear's meal? *No!* Am I *going* to be a bear's meal? *No!* So am I going to *act* like a bear's meal? *No!* When you have the right feelings inside you, they come out in the way you act."

"Right," Lily said thoughtfully.

"But don't worry too much. If we just walk naturally, and keep talking to let them know we're coming, they'll probably stay away in the first place."

"Right," Lily said again, louder than usual, peering into the trees. "Let's do that!"

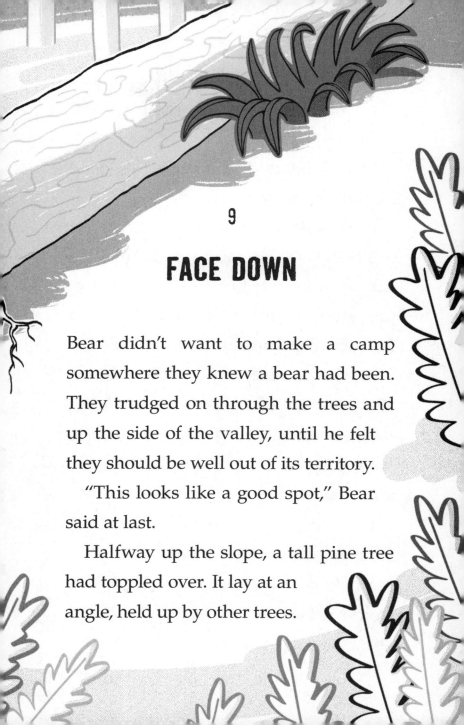

9

FACE DOWN

Bear didn't want to make a camp somewhere they knew a bear had been. They trudged on through the trees and up the side of the valley, until he felt they should be well out of its territory.

"This looks like a good spot," Bear said at last.

Halfway up the slope, a tall pine tree had toppled over. It lay at an angle, held up by other trees.

Its roots had torn out of the ground and left a pit at its base, making a natural shelter.

"That's handy," Lily said. "It's done most of the work for us."

Bear smiled. "And it's in a perfect position. It's south facing, so it's had the sun on it for most of the day to warm the ground. We're about a hundred feet above the valley floor, so cold air from the mountains will sink past us. The soil's dry because all the water has drained downward. There are a couple more touches we can do and then it'll be perfect."

First they cut branches from nearby trees with a machete Bear produced from his backpack.

Lily was the right size to get in close to the trunks through the needles, and find the best branches.

"Make them slim," Bear said, "about as thick as your arm, and three feet long."

They put the first branches down on the floor as insulation from the cold ground. The fir tree branches were flat, so Bear and Lily could lay them one on top of the other. Then they made a roof, propping overlapping branches between the ground and the tree roots. The needles grew close together, so the shelter was now windproof and waterproof. Lily remembered the first day of camp, when everyone had made shelters out of what they could find in the woods. She would certainly have won a prize if she'd made something like this!

Lily and Bear climbed into the pit to investigate their work from below. Lily looked proudly up at the covering. Everything was warm and piney and full of green light.

"This'll do nicely." Bear smiled. "And now, for our last job, we can make a fire to cook on."

"Fantastic!" said Lily. The energy bars had kept them going, but after a day of walking, she was more than ready for some hot food.

Just then, a deep, throaty growl made her leap out of her skin, and a powerful claw tore through the roof. Branches tumbled down into the pit on top of Bear.

A massive bear covered with dark, shaggy fur glared down at them through the hole in the roof.

A gale of hot breath hit Lily in the face as it roared. It stank of rotting meat.

Lily stood, petrified, rooted to the spot.

"Lily! Black bear! Make yourself big!"

Bear was struggling to get up through the branches. In a couple of seconds he would be free, but Lily knew they might not have a couple of seconds.

This bear meant business.

What had Bear said about black bears?
Face them down.

So Lily pulled together every scrap of courage and shouted louder than she'd ever shouted before.

"I am *not* going to be your meal!"

The bear reared up onto its hind legs. Its front paws were still raised, like a boxer's hands. A boxer with claws as long as dinner knives.

"Lily!" Bear was heaving a branch off his leg. "Stand tall! Shout!"

So Lily jumped up to the edge of the pit. She leaped as high as she could, and she flung her arms out as wide as they would go.

"*Ra-a-ah!*"

The bear roared
back at her. Its
teeth looked like
they could tear
through steel.
Lily's heart pounded. This animal could
bite her in two without trying.

Lily always liked to stay quiet. But
now, for the first time in her life,
making herself heard had become
a matter of life and death.

So she screamed louder than she
had ever thought possible.

"*RA-A-A-AH!*"

The bear wavered on its
back legs.

Lily wasn't finished. She ran

forward, waving her arms and screaming her lungs out.

The bear grunted. It turned and dropped down to all fours. Then it mooched away. It shot her a final, grumpy look before it disappeared into the trees.

Bear had pulled himself out and was right behind her.

"Wow!" he gasped. "You nailed it, Lily. You were absolutely terrifying!"

Lily grinned. "Thanks!" She was panting hard, but she felt good about herself. She had spoken up and faced down something really scary.

"You really found

your voice, Lily. That was such awesome work. But maybe we'll pick a different spot for a camp," Bear added.

Lily looked sadly at the remains of their shelter. They had put a lot of hard work into it and it seemed a shame to leave it. But it would seem even more of a shame to be eaten by a hungry bear.

Bear's backpack was still buried in the wreckage.

"I'll get it," Lily said. "I'm smaller." She would be able to duck under the fallen branches more easily. Besides, she was feeling so much better. Now that all that fear she'd been carrying around with her had gone, she felt so much lighter.

Lily jumped down and crouched under a branch. The backpack was just out of reach, so she started to crawl.

Suddenly she tumbled forward. The ground vanished, just like when she had arrived on the mountain.

This time, Lily didn't hit solid stones, and she didn't roll very far.

"Hey, Lily, get a move on! I need to get out too."

Mia was kneeling in the hatch of the bubble, waiting for Lily to get out of the way.

Bear and everything else had vanished.

10

NEEDING TO BE SAID

"Wow! I'm really sorry!"

Joe tottered out of the boys' bubble behind Omar. He looked really upset.

"That was totally my fault," he said.

"What happened, Joe?" Mia asked, rubbing a big bruise on her arm and glaring at him.

It was all coming back to Lily. The crash. The bubble going out of control. Mia not being strapped in. It certainly wasn't *all* Joe's fault. And Mia should know that.

"Are you all okay?" a grown-up voice called. "What happened?"

The leader was running down the slope towards them. Lily noticed she did it like Bear, leaning backward and putting her weight on her heels.

Where *was* Bear? Lily looked around again. Had she hit her head badly and just imagined everything?

"Totally my fault," Joe said again. "Omar was telling me to go right, but ... uh ... I got confused with left and right. I'm sorry." He looked at Lily and Mia. "Sorry we knocked into you. Sorry you got hurt, Mia."

"That's okay," Mia said, still rubbing her arm.

Lily narrowed her eyes, but she kept quiet. This time she wasn't keeping quiet just to avoid making a fuss. There was something she needed to say, but she only needed to say it to Mia. It wouldn't be kind to say it in front of everyone.

"Okay." The leader thought for a moment. "Boys, let's see your left hands."

Omar and Joe did as they were asked. Lily noticed that Joe waited to see which hand Omar held up before he did the same.

"Perfect!" the leader said. "You're both wearing watches on your left wrist. So, from now on, instead of left and right, you can say 'watch' and 'not-watch.'"

Joe's unhappy face immediately vanished behind a smile.

"Sure, I can do that!"

"Yeah, cool," Omar said brightly.

"Right. All of you push your bubbles back up, and we'll try again, shall we?"

Lily and Mia got together behind their bubble to push it back up the slope. Lily bit her lip and then took the plunge. She needed to speak up and she needed to do it now.

"Why do you think Joe owned up to the crash being his fault?" Lily asked.

Mia shrugged.

"Dunno. I suppose it was quite brave. But it was all his fault."

Once, Lily would have left it there. But they'd gotten hurt not because of the crash, but because of Mia not paying attention to instructions. What if someone got really hurt later on because Lily didn't speak up?

Lily remembered Bear's advice about speaking up: *If it's true, and if it's useful, it needs to be said.* And right now, Mia was the one it needed to be said to.

"Mia, we wouldn't have gone so out of control if you'd strapped yourself in right!"

Mia looked at Lily in surprise, and her mouth opened and closed a few times.

But then she smiled.

"You're right," she agreed. "I'm sorry."

Lily was pleased, and when they got to rerun their race, Mia strapped herself into the bubble the right way. The boys stayed on course too, with the watch/non-watch directions. The bubbles knocked into each other a couple of times, and into a few trees, but that was how it was supposed to be. They crossed the finishing line in a tie.

At lunch, Lily loaded her tray and headed for a table. Mia and Omar were behind her, both chatting about their afternoon activities.

"Hey, Lily, I think you dropped this." Mia plonked something onto her table. Then she sat down next to her, and carried on chatting with Omar.

Lily's heart thudded.

It was the fossil that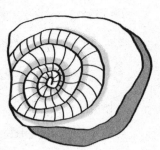
she had gotten at the
top of the mountain.
The one that had
been exposed when the
cliff collapsed in front of her and Bear.

But that had just been a dream because
she'd hit her head. Hadn't it?

Lily thought about Bear's advice,
and her new confidence in speaking
up. Perhaps she really *had* been on the
mountain.

But how would she have gotten there?

Lily tried to remember exactly how
things had gone that morning. It had been
so whirling and confusing, bouncing
around inside that bubble. Even the
compass had gotten confused. Lily

remembered its strange five directions, and the spinning needle.

She took the compass out of her pocket. It only showed four directions now, and the needle was pointing north.

Hmm, Lily thought. Was it all the same thing? The dizziness and the compass spinning? Did it have something to do with her adventure with Bear?

"Hey, Lily – earth to Lily!" Joe said. Lily realized he'd been talking to her. "Where did you get the chips?" Joe asked.

Lily pointed at the snack table.

"That table, on the end at the right," she said.

"Cool, thanks."

Joe set off for the left end. Halfway there, he changed direction.

And Lily, who had been wondering

if Mia would like the compass, changed her mind in a split second. She was suddenly sure that Joe needed it more. Perhaps he could learn something from Bear too.

So, when Joe got back to the table, Lily pushed the compass across to him.

"Hey, Joe, would you like this?"

Joe scowled at her.

"Hey! Why do you think I need a compass? Because I get lost so easily?"

Lily realized that he had taken her gesture the wrong way. She wasn't trying to make a joke.

She could have just said, "Never mind," and walked away. But Lily knew this was something else that needed to be said. She needed to speak up because she was sure Bear really could help Joe, and the compass had something to do with it.

"I'm not teasing, Joe," she said. "Really. It's just it's a pretty cool compass, honestly. I think you'll like it. Just consider it a gift."

The End

Bear Grylls got the taste for adventure at a young age from his father, a former Royal Marine. After school, Bear joined the Reserve SAS, then went on to become one of the youngest people ever to climb Mount Everest, just two years after breaking his back in three places during a parachute jump.

Among other adventures he has led expeditions to the Arctic and the Antarctic, crossed oceans and set world records in skydiving and paragliding.

Bear is also a bestselling author and the host of television programs such as *Survival School* and *The Island*.

He has shared his survival skills with people all over the world, and has taken many famous movie stars and sports stars on adventures – and even President Barack Obama!

Bear Grylls is Chief Scout to the UK Scouting Association, encouraging young people to have great adventures, follow their dreams and to look after their friends. Bear is also honorary Colonel to the Royal Marine Commandos.

When Bear's not traveling the world, he lives with his wife and three sons on a barge in London, or on an island off the coast of Wales.

Find out more at **www.beargrylls.com**

BRILLIANT BEASTLY BEARS

DID YOU KNOW?

•Black bears live in Europe and North America, where winters can be cold. They make their dens in caves, burrows or places with good shelter, and feed on grasses, fruits, nuts and seeds, as well as fish.

•Bears take very, very long naps in winter, feeding on body fat they have built up in summer and autumn, and staying in their dens.

•Black bears aren't always black! Their coats have two layers of fur, and can be blue-gray or blue-black or even lighter brown. There's even a black bear with white fur called the "Spirit Bear"! The first layer of their coat keeps them warm, and the next layer keeps them dry.

•Teddy bears are said to be named after President Theodore "Teddy" Roosevelt, who refused to shoot a black bear on a hunting trip in 1902.

•Winnipeg was a famous female black bear who lived at the London Zoo. The author A.A. Milne's son, Christopher Robin, changed the name of his own teddy bear from "Edward Bear" to "Winnie-the-Pooh," inspiring the famous stories.